Zip-Pea's Shadow

One day while I was digging in my garden, I discovered a village of little flowerpots. In this village lived the Poddington Peas.

The Peas soon became my friends, and began to tell me stories of their adventures. In return I promised to keep the secret of where they lived.

This is one of the many stories they told me.

Zip-Pea was the fastest Pea in Poddington. He was so fast that if you blinked you might just miss him as he zoomed around at high speed.

There was only one thing that could keep up with Zip-Pea, and that was his little black shadow.

Zip-Pea was racing round Poddington as usual when suddenly he skidded to a halt in a cloud of dust. As the dust cleared, Zip-Pea stood still — which was very hard for him to do. Then he realised that something dreadful had happened.

Zip-Pea's shadow was missing. He looked all round him, but it was completely gone.

Zip-Pea was looking very puzzled when Slop-Pea, the messiest Pea in Poddington, came strolling up.

'Morning,' he said, and when he saw how worried Zip-Pea looked, he added 'What's the matter – you lost your shadow or something?'

'Yes, as a matter of fact I have,' said poor Zip-Pea.

'Cheer-up, Zip-Pea,' said Slop-Pea. 'Don't worry about your shadow. If you stand in front of that wall, I will paint you a new one!'

So Zip-Pea stood in front of the wall while Slop-Pea slopped on some black paint to make him a new shadow.

Zip-Pea was very pleased with his new shadow – it looked just like his old one. He thanked Slop-Pea and zoomed off, but the painted shadow didn't follow.

'Well that's no good,' said Zip-Pea. 'Shadows are supposed to keep up with you! Slop-Pea's paint can't be runny enough. Or perhaps it's extra quick drying. I will just have to find my old shadow.'

And with that he zoomed on his way.

Zip-Pea sped all over Poddington in search of his little black shadow. At last he skidded to a halt at Sweet Pea's house. He looked through the window and saw her playing a shadow game with Hap-Pea.

'That's a pretty shadow,' said Zip-Pea. 'You haven't seen mine, have you?'

'Your shadow, Zip-Pea? Sorry – we haven't seen a trace of it.'

Poor Zip-Pea zoomed off again.

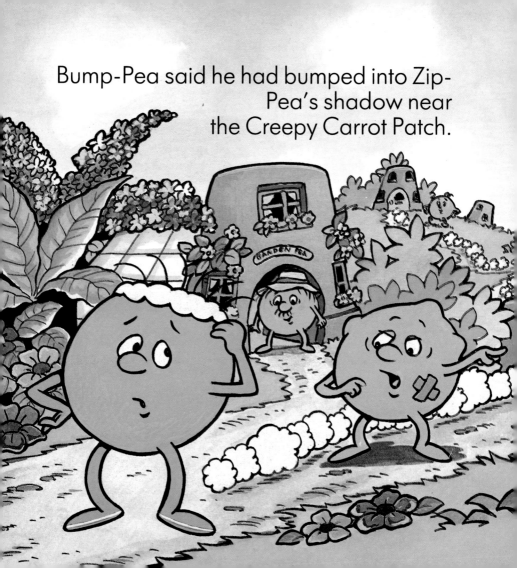

Bump-Pea said he had bumped into Zip-Pea's shadow near the Creepy Carrot Patch.

'Oh dear!' thought Zip-Pea, 'If my shadow wanders off into the dark mists of Creepy Castle, it will be lost forever.'

Zip-Pea was about to zip up the Rockery to dark and gloomy Creepy Castle, when he felt a tap on his shoulder.

It was G-Pea, Poddington's very own doctor.

'Phew!' panted G-Pea. 'You're a hard Pea to find, Zip-Pea. I've been all over Poddington looking for you.'

'I've got someone special waiting to meet you at my surgery,' said G-Pea. 'I think you're in for a surprise!'

Zip-Pea led the way to the surgery, while G-Pea tried as hard as he could to keep up.

When G-Pea arrived, out of breath, Zip-Pea was leaning on the door, waiting for him.

'There you are at last!' said Zip-Pea. 'Hurry up and open the door – I love surprises!'

G-Pea opened his surgery door and let Zip-Pea in. There was a figure stretched out on the couch, looking very sorry for itself.

It was Zip-Pea's shadow!

'What are you doing here?' asked Zip-Pea. 'I've been looking all over Poddington for you. I've been really worried!'

G-Pea took Zip-Pea aside. 'Your shadow is tired out with trying to keep up with you. If you want to stay attached to him, you'll have to slow down a bit.'

G-Pea gave Zip-Pea a prescription which read:

'SLOW DOWN – three times a day.'

Zip-Pea did not like the idea of slowing down three times a day. But he liked the idea of running around without his shadow even less.

So Zip-Pea shook hands with his shadow and promised he would take G-Pea's advice.

'I'll do my best to slow down.'

Zip-Pea and his little black shadow were both happy to be back together again. They thanked G-Pea and zipped off a little more slowly than usual. Only a little more slowly.

If you want to know if Zip-Pea slowed down three times a day, you'll have to ask his shadow. Or of course you could ask Zip-Pea — the fastest Pea in Poddington.